WooWee
the Cat and
Almost Grumpy Pat

Forever Friends

Written and Illustrated by

Kelley-Ann Heslop

◆ FriesenPress

Suite 300 - 990 Fort St
Victoria, BC, V8V 3K2
Canada

www.friesenpress.com

ISBN
978-1-5255-1291-9 (Hardcover)
978-1-5255-1292-6 (Paperback)
978-1-5255-1293-3 (eBook)

1. JUVENILE FICTION, ANIMALS, CATS1

Distributed to the trade by The Ingram Book Company

This book is for
my dear husband.
Almost Grumpy Pat Heslop,
my inspiration,
my best friend,
my greatest love.

In the beginning, maybe even before **that**, there lived a **lonely man** named **Almost Grumpy Pat.**

While he sat like a lump on his overused **chair**, the ding-dong of his doorbell rang out through the **air**.

As he opened his front door he could not believe his eyes, there was a stray cat on his step, and that was a

surprise.

Almost Grumpy Pat began to humph, he just about yelled SCAT!

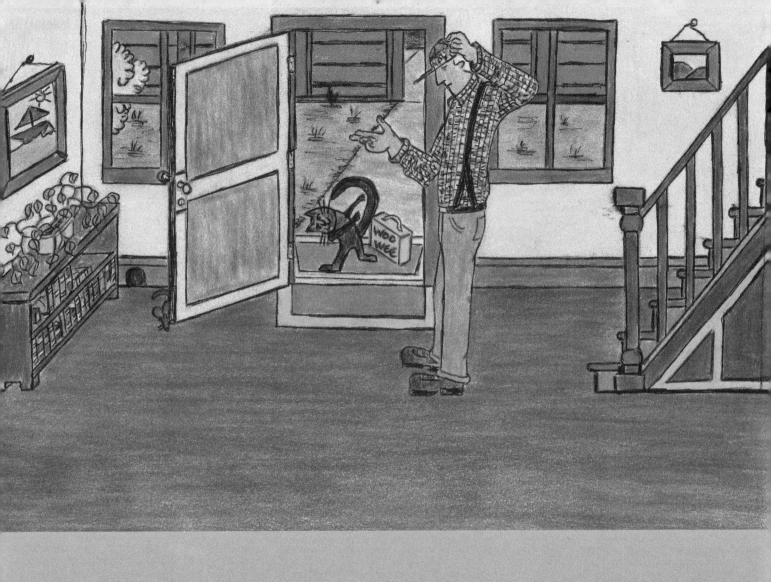

But the kitty politely
bowed and said,
"I'm your new cat."

"My name is

WooWee,

and I'm choosing you.
You're my new owner! How
do you do?"

He picked up his suitcase
and showed himself in,
as Almost Grumpy Pat's
frown turned into a grin.

Poor little WooWee had been living on the street. It got really cold at night and he had nothing to eat. He needed someone to look after him, especially when he got

scared.

WooWee chose Almost Grumpy Pat because he **felt** that he **cared**.

Cat Rescue took WooWee to the Animal Clinic to make sure he was okay, and Almost Grumpy Pat's **heart** broke in half as they drove him away.

When WooWee was ready for **foster care** Almost Grumpy Pat was full of glee,

"I'll take care of him until
you find his

forever
home,

because I think he chose me!"

Almost Grumpy Pat's home was just like the one WooWee pictured in his mind.

As he unpacked his little suitcase he said, "Thank you for being so kind."

He showed Almost Grumpy Pat his Bucket List, which he rolled out on the floor.

"These are all the things I want to do that I have never done **before**."

While Pat dreamed almost grumpy dreams something jumped up on his **bed**. "Wake up, wake up!" WooWee repeated. "WAKE UP **SLEEPY HEAD!**"

"It's time to seize the day!" he declared, "I mean, lets go out and **play**.

Life is meant for
living and our
adventures
start today.["]

Almost Grumpy Pat went outside and got his bike out of the shed. While WooWee found a flowerpot and made a helmet for his head. At the lake they went swimming and did cannonballs off the pier, and Almost Grumpy Pat thought to himself, I haven't had this much

fun in years.

They built a sandcastle fit for a queen, with a moat that went all the way around. WooWee imagined the people living inside; their King was wearing a crown. At lunch time they took a break to enjoy the picnic lunch they brought.

Dill pickles and boiled eggs are very **yummy**, they really hit the **spot.**

As Almost Grumpy Pat
stared into the campfire he
remembered that he used to
feel sad.
This little kitty changed his
whole life, he was the

best
friend

he'd ever had.

He looked at WooWee singing his heart out while strumming his little guitar, and smiled every time he sang out of tune, because WooWee thought he was a rock star.

They went fishing the next morning and Almost Grumpy Pat got a **bite**, but the stinky old boot he reeled in did not put up much of a **fight**. Then WooWee caught a beautiful fish and **chose** to set it

free,

he said, "Lets keep the boot
and plant flowers in it for
everyone to see."

WooWee pretended he was mountain climbing as a rock began to slide.

When it hit the ground it split in half and they found a fossil hidden inside.

Almost Grumpy Pat said, "Jump into my arms," and WooWee began to

purr.

He leaped off the cliff
and yelled, "GERONIMO!"
which was his favourite
jumping word.

They took the fossil back
to their campsite to have a
better look.

It was exactly like the
prehistoric plant in their
Fossils for Dummies
book.

WooWee was very excited
because fossils were on his
Bucket List.

"Oh my goodness," he cheerfully announced, "we're paleontologists!"

When they got home from their camping trip they put everything away, and that was when WooWee said, "I really wish I could stay."

"I'm glad of that," said Almost Grumpy Pat. "I believe you and I are meant to be.

You're so awesome and a joy to be around.

We are a
family."

Almost Grumpy Pat called
Cat Rescue and said,
"We have no idea who's
adopting who.
So we are going to adopt
each other, because that's
what we want to do."
After signing a lot of
paperwork they were given a
certificate at the end,

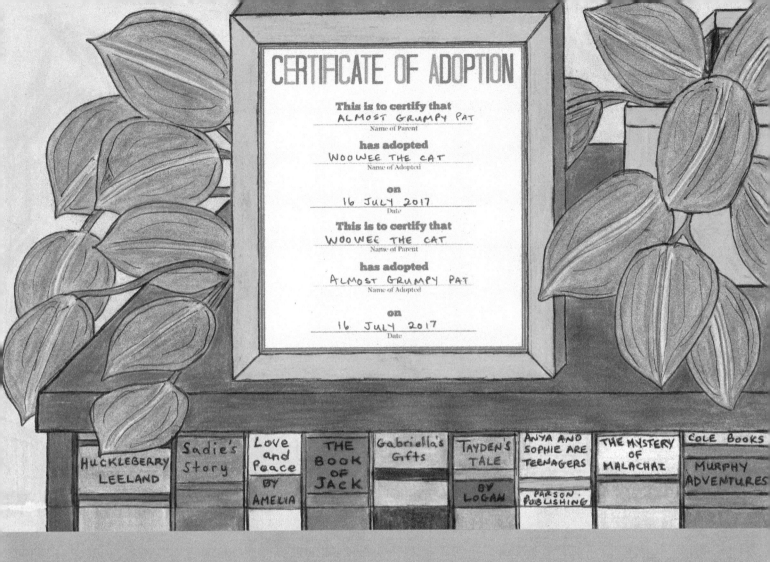

CERTIFICATE OF ADOPTION

This is to certify that
ALMOST GRUMPY PAT
Name of Parent

has adopted
WOOWEE THE CAT
Name of Adopted

on
16 JULY 2017
Date

This is to certify that
WOOWEE THE CAT
Name of Parent

has adopted
ALMOST GRUMPY PAT
Name of Adopted

on
16 JULY 2017
Date

HUCKLEBERRY LEELAND

Sadie's Story

Love and Peace BY AMELIA

THE BOOK OF JACK

Gabriella's Gifts

TAYDEN'S TALE

BY LOGAN

ANYA AND SOPHIE ARE TEENAGERS

PARSON PUBLISHING

THE MYSTERY OF MALACHAI

COLE BOOKS

MURPHY ADVENTURES

and that is how WooWee found his forever home where he lives with his forever friend.

Almost Grumpy Pat bought a present for WooWee, which made him hoot and **holler**.

It was a chair exactly like his, only this one was a wee bit **smaller**.

"I love it! I love it! **I LOVE IT!**" WooWee exclaimed, as Almost Grumpy Pat's heart filled with **delight**.

Then they danced around the room, whirling and twirling, celebrating their special night.

Later on when the sun went down and the stars came out to play, WooWee the Cat and Almost Grumpy Pat talked about their day.

He tucked WooWee in bed and softly said,

"I love you more than you can ever know."

"Goodnight, sleep tight, my little furry **friend**. I can't wait until **tomorrow**."

Oooops!

I just about forgot.

Marlo the mouse said, "I'm worried about a cat in the house," as she gobbled up her **chop suey**.

"There's no need to fear, **my dear**," replied Charlie, her spouse.

"He told me his name
is WooWee."

The End.
(Of book one)

CPSIA information can be obtained
at www.ICGtesting.com
Printed in the USA
LVHW01s1602281217
561038LV00004B/4/P